SONG OF THE HORSE

by Richard Kennedy · illustrated by Marcia Sewall

A UNICORN BOOK · E. P. DUTTON   NEW YORK

Library of Congress Cataloging in Publication Data

Kennedy, Richard, date   Song of the horse.
(A Unicorn book)

Summary: A girl and her horse feel a great love for each other
and experience powerful, consuming feelings when riding together.
[1. Horses—Fiction]   I. Sewall, Marcia.   II. Title
PZ7.K385So   1981   [Fic]   81-5043
ISBN 0-525-39675-6   AACR2

Published in the United States by Elsevier-Dutton
Publishing Co., Inc., 2 Park Avenue, New York, N.Y. 10016

Published simultaneously in Canada by Clarke,
Irwin & Company Limited, Toronto and Vancouver

Editor: Emilie McLeod   Designer: Riki Levinson

Printed in the U.S.A.   First Edition   10 9 8 7 6 5 4 3 2 1

for Monica O'Keefe Marburg

Out of the house I go and down the hill. The sun shines on the green meadow, yellow flowers, blue sky, white clouds and brown path as I run to the center of all the world of color, the small red barn. And inside there, in the dim light, is a horse who is the center, the focus, the very heart of all horsedom, and he belongs to me. He is waiting for me. He is always waiting for me, standing still and thinking about me. Standing upright in his sleep he dreams about me, and he never dreams of anything else. Or if he does, he doesn't remember it. There is a picture of me inside his head that never goes away. Ever and always I am on his mind. Hardly anything is real to him but me. I think it a wonder that a horse can be so single-minded.

When he looks over the top of his stall into the sky, he sees my face in the clouds. He sees me in rainbows and shadows and hears my voice in the rain and the wind. The light of my eyes is in the stars, sun and moon. And now he sees me coming to him, and he snorts. That is his name for me. Now he blows through his lips, saying that he is ready to run, and he stomps his feet and runs his chest against his gate. He can hardly wait.

We stand face-to-face and I touch his nose. We look at each other. Spirit is his name. I say, "Spirit." He snorts my name again. It is the only name he knows, the name of all names to him—the name of apples and soap, of oats and clear water, of brushing his mane, the feel of my hand at his mouth, my gripping legs on his ribs. There is no name but me.

I open his gate and go into his stall. I put an arm over his neck as I reach for the bridle and reins. He shivers and moves. Naturally he is excited. He spends his life waiting for these moments. I must be careful he doesn't step on my foot.

"Easy, now," I say, patting him. One of us must remain calm.

O chest of Spirit, O neck, O mane, O jaw and belly and rump and tail. I loop his head with the rein. O leg and hoof of Spirit, O smell and power of Spirit.

"Open your mouth for the bit, you big dummy!"

Out we go and I swing onto his bare back. No horse and no rider
have ever balanced so perfectly as Spirit and myself. I could ride him
blindfolded, standing up, on one foot, tiptoe, with my arms out-
stretched. I think I could, anyway. We walk, and this is a difficult
time for him. We cannot run until we pass the gate, and he can
hardly stand it.

He loves me to be on his back and he barely walks straight for nervousness and excitement. He loves the feel of my hands on his neck, the weight of my body, and the touch of my heels. Sometimes I don't understand how he can love me so much. Sometimes I think it is a kind of craziness.

His sides are like breathing mountains and he blows through his nose like a locomotive. His legs are like mighty wheels that have been made straight, his tail like spouting steam, and his eyes are like shining lights. We are almost at the gate. All his nerves are like the trembling strings of a great instrument. He waits for my touch to run, walking almost sideways for joy and eagerness. And here is the gate.

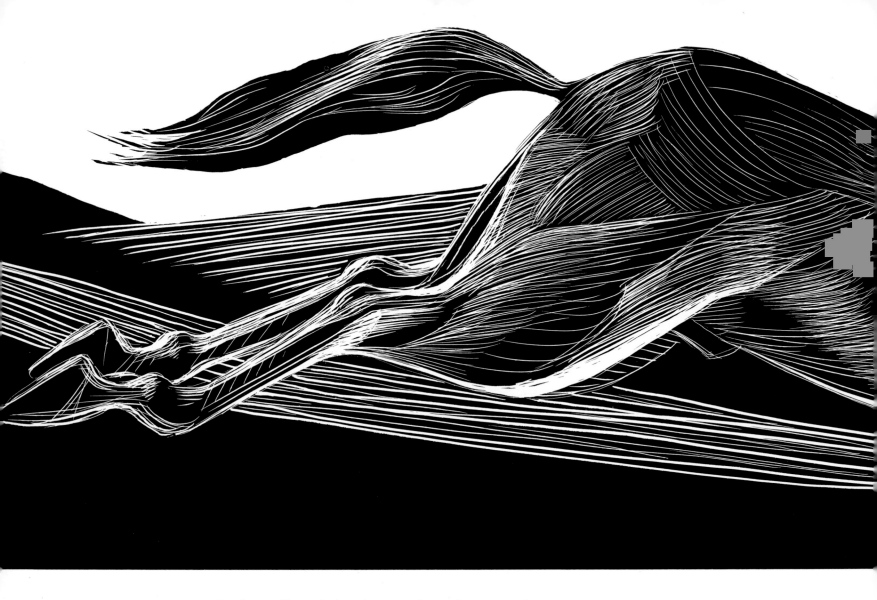

"Go!" I yell and slap his neck and dig my heels at his heaving sides
and grip my knees to his ribs.

And we go!

O, my explosion of a horse; O, my lovely, heavenly horse; O,
my God who made my horse and me! Ears like wands, hoofs like

diamonds, breath like a volcano, mane like a storm in my face, we charge into the wind with our mouths open. We eat and drink the wind, we live on speed and thunder, we see by lightning flashes, and our charging gives birth to hurricanes and tornadoes. All underground creatures think we are an earthquake.

Moles and mice rush from their holes to see what great event is happening, but we are gone. We are a phantom, a ghost. We are wonderful to all things, beautiful to the earth, happy to all things, and the sound of our running is like a shout of wonder and awe. We run so fast that the trees look forever different after we pass. Fence posts are struck dumb by our speed. People who see us remember us only in dreams. The sheep argue about our existence. The slow-eyed grazing cows say we are fictional. The chickens think we are supernatural.

Faster and faster—and we are as close as clasped hands, sharing each other completely, our pounding flesh and flashing blood, striking bones and beating brains—crossing and weaving ourselves together, knowing all of each other we ride madly into secrets and leave the shreds of mysteries behind us like a wake.

We lick the earth like a dark flame. All things know themselves as we approach and forget themselves as we pass. Nothing is the same forever after when the dust has settled behind us. Every blade of grass and clod of dirt remembers us, and the dust talks to the dust and tells stories and legends of our passing. Beetles and crickets think we are God.

All along the dreadful trail of our passing we leave the worship of horses. Distant hills and fields adore us and despair they have not the indelible print of our feet on their great slow bodies. And we run faster yet, a gigantic and vanishing sight.

We know everything! What we hear is all there is to hear. The
rushing wind and the voice of the earth tell us all there is to tell.
Thigh and bone, muscle and the rising heat of flesh and blood. We

feel all there is to feel. We are the center of all senses. We see faster than the speed of light. The shouting and cheering world surrounds us all about. Faster, faster!

We run past the wind, past the shouting of praises, past the cheering and into stillness, past sound and into silence. We run past time and age and we run past our running and into slow motion. We run as in a dream—lifted away from our senses, frozen and flying in the heart of a crystal ball—and everything is revealed. I have no sisters, I have no brother. There is no barn and no house up the path, and I have no mother or father. We run into a place where all is perfectly still, and there is no difference in anything and no sameness in anything, and in this great empty moment, a song is singing.

The song has words that are ancient and strange, and music like newborn water, tumbling all together, but I can't remember any of it. It is entirely beautiful. There is not too little of it and not too much. Nothing is left over. It is all perfect.

Sometimes my heart beats to the rhythm of it, and then I stop what I am doing and stand perfectly still, trying to hear the words and music of it. But I can't.

Only when I ride Spirit do I hear that song. Sometimes I fear I'll never hear it again.

Then comes an explosion, and we are overtaken by the sound
of pounding hoofs, and we are back in time and slowing down.
Wet and steaming, walking and panting, we go back to the barn.

I dry Spirit and comb him and feed him and talk to him. He hates to see me go. He is never tired of being with me. When I shut his gate he stares at me with a long look in his eyes, and he talks to me. I hear it in my mind. He says, "If you do not come back I will die of sorrow. I will not eat or sleep or open my eyes ever again, but I will lie down and breathe slower and slower until I stop breathing, because I could never live without you."

Then I put my cheek against his face and hold his great head and say to him, "O, Spirit." It comforts him.

I go out of the barn and walk up the path to the house. When I turn, he is looking at me. "No one will understand," he says, and shakes his head from side to side. And I walk away. I am sad because everything will be boring to him until I return, and he can't tell anyone how he feels. I stop for a moment on the path, listening, but I hear nothing. Then I go into the house.

Mother says to me, "Are you hungry?"

"I don't know," I say. "I guess so." I sit down and look out the window.

"Did you take Spirit for a run?"

"Uh-huh."

"Did you enjoy yourself?"

"It was all right."